S0-FDJ-167

Katarína Macurová

HENRY THE SNAIL

Albatros

The last rain was still dripping from the leaves . . .

. . . when Henry the snail first saw the light of day.

He came straight out of his shell,
eager to climb, like all the other snails.

"There's nothing to it,"
Henry told himself.
"You just stick to the stalk
with your slime . . ."

". . . and push yourself up."

So he gripped hard . . .   . . . using first one tentacle . . .

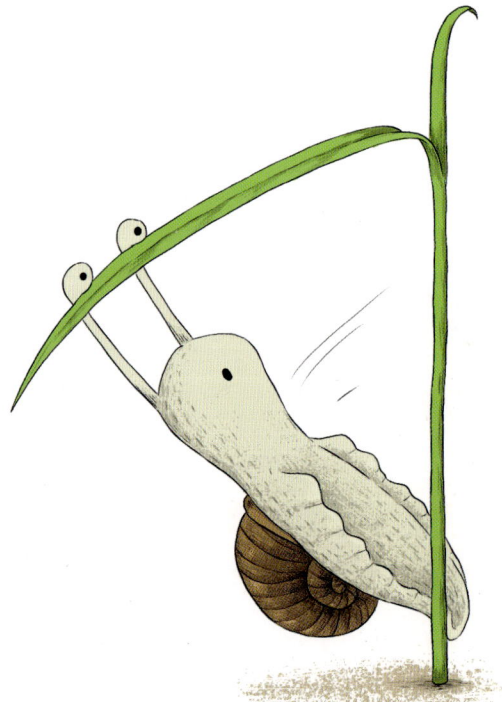

. . . then the other . . .   . . . and . . .

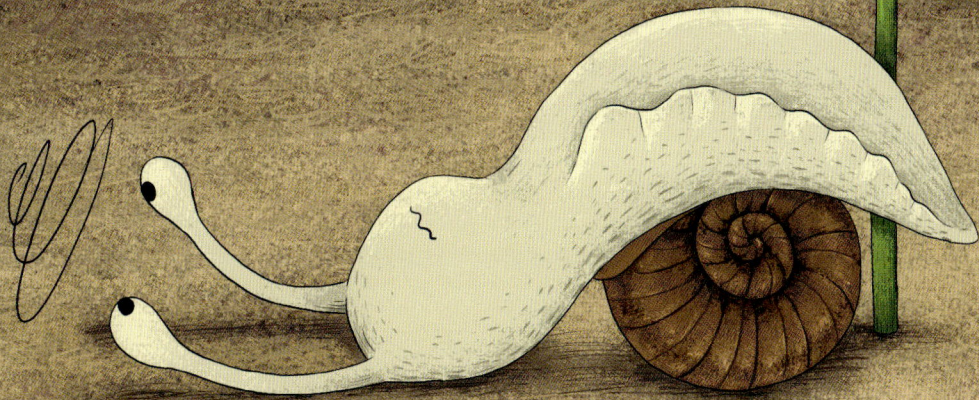

Because Henry the snail
had no slime.

Whenever he
tried to hold on to
the stalk . . .

. . . he always came
sliding down.

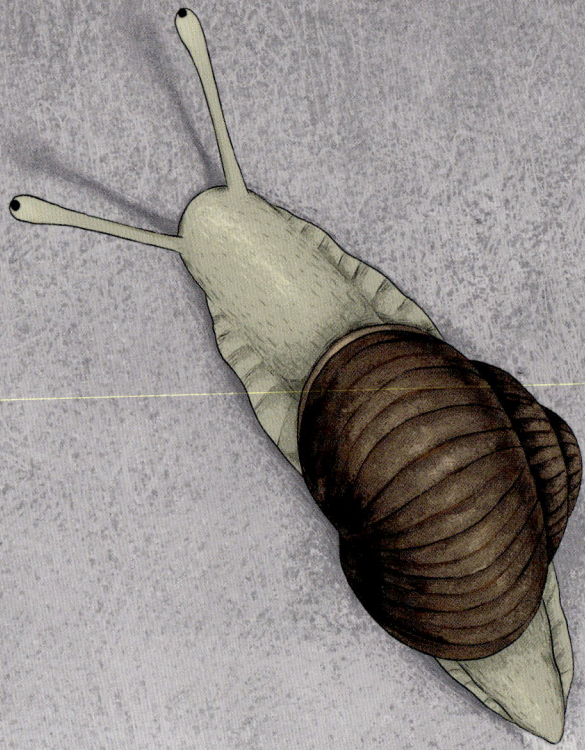

He could move only along the ground.

"How I wish I could climb upwards!" he sighed.
"I would climb all the way to the top."

Early the next morning, he bathed in honey,
to make his belly sticky.

This turned out not to be
the best idea.

Then he found a drop of fresh tree sap . . .

. . . which was much too sticky.

"Nothing works like slime," he said, disappointed.

"But maybe, if I were strong enough,
I could make it to the top without it."

So every day he exercised . . .

. . . by dragging pebbles . . .

. . . lifting peas . . .

. . . and balancing peach pits
on his belly.

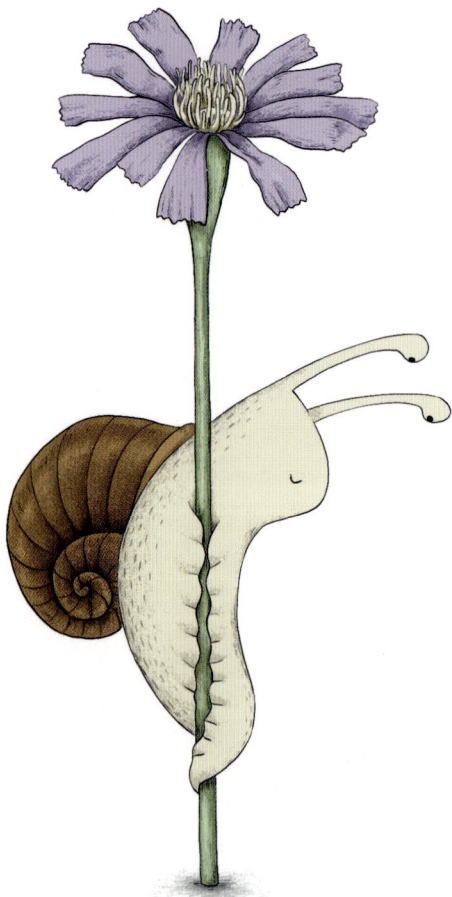

Soon, he was strong enough
to hold on to the stalk.
And this was no ordinary hold.

He could hang upside down
and turn.

He could bend like a leaf.

He could even do
a headstand on a cherry.

At last the time had come for him to climb
the tallest flower in the garden.

He took a deep breath and began to climb . . .

. . . but halfway up, he came to a stop.
He couldn't go on.

"I've always wanted a shell like yours," said a smiling slug, before asking Henry if he needed help.

When Henry reached the top, he cried, "What a brilliant view!"

After that, Henry climbed just as the other snails and slugs did.

Whenever he ran out of energy, he always
found a willing helper. He saw no shame in that.
In fact, he was proud he could do something . . .

. . . none of the others could do.

But Henry also wanted to help the others. So he started teaching everyone else his stunts—and they did their best to learn.

Soon, they became quite good at them . . .

. . . and so . . .

. . . they set up a snail circus together.
Can you guess what they called it?

Henry's Circus, of course!

© B4U Publishing for Albatros,
an imprint of Albatros Media Group, 2023
5. května 1746/22, Prague 4, Czech Republic
Written & illustrated by Katarína Macurová
Translated by Andrew Oakland
Edited by Scott Alexander Jones

Printed in China by Leo Paper Group

All rights reserved.

Reproduction of any content is strictly prohibited
without the written permission of the rights holders.

albatros